WINFIELD PUBLIC LIBRARY
T 72155

P9-DGC-039

Miss Bindergarten Has a WILD DAY in Kindergarten

by JOSEPH SLATE
illustrated by ASHLEY WOLFF

Dutton Children's Books · New York

CIP Data is available.

Published in the United States by Dutton Children's Books,
a division of Penguin Young Readers Group
345 Hudson Street, New York, New York 10014
www.penguin.com
First Edition · Manufactured in China
ISBN 0-525-47084-0
10 9 8 7 6 5 4 3 2 1

For Marge Haganman, a teacher for over 42 years, who loves the good days and laughs at the wild in Wapello. And to my great-nephew Ensign Joe Sheridan—wild anchors aweigh.

J.S.

For Amy Whitcomb, who makes Miss Bindergarten look tame

A.W.

Adam throws his hat too high.

Brenda bursts in late.

Christopher says he has to go—
he really cannot wait.

Miss Bindergarten begins

a wild day in kindergarten.

Danny tends his droopy beans.

Emily spies some ants.

Franny lifts her dress and shouts,
"I love my fancy pants!"

Miss Bindergarten has

a wild day in kindergarten.

Gwen falls off the step stool.

Henry just won't share.

Ian sadly tells Miss B,
"We didn't mean to tear."

Miss Bindergarten and the librarian

have a wild day in kindergarten.

Jessie drops the bug jar.

Kiki cuts her thumb.

Lenny says, "Uh-oh, Miss B,
we need the nurse to come."

Miss Bindergarten and the nurse

have a wild day in kindergarten.

Matty checks a chrysalis.

Noah drops his rock.

Ophelia's oozy painting is sticking to her smock.

Patricia trips and flips her tray.

Quentin overloads.

Raffie Mack soaks Sara
when his apple juice explodes.

Miss Bindergarten and the cafeteria helper

have a wild day in kindergarten.

Tommy dumps in too much dirt.

Ursula's seed pack rips.

Vicky pours in waaaaaaay too much,
and the cardboard carton drips.

Now Miss Bindergarten and the custodian

have a wild day in kindergarten.

Wanda whacks the principal.

Xavier skins his knee.

Yolanda says,
"Come look, Miss B!—

GIRLS
Milkweed

Zach set the butterflies free."

Miss Bindergarten and everyone enjoy

an even wilder day in kindergarten.

"Sometimes even a wild day," says Miss B,
"turns up something wonderful to see."

Life cycle of a PLANT
RAIN
SUN
SOIL
SPROUT
ROOTS
SEED
FLOWER
LEAF
LEAF
PLANT

Life cycle
of a
BUTTERFLY
LEAF
Milkweed
Caterpillar
Chrysalis
EGG
Butterfly

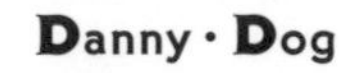

Adam · Alligator | Brenda · Beaver | Christopher · Cat | Danny · Dog | Emily · Elephant | Franny · Frog

Gwen · Gorilla | Henry · Hippopotamus | Ian · Iguana | Jessie · Jaguar | Kiki · Kangaroo | Lenny · Lion

Miss Bindergarten's WILD DAY Kindergarten

Matty · Moose | Noah · Newt | Ophelia · Otter | Patricia · Pig

Quentin · Quokka | Raffie · Rhinoceros | Sara · Squirrel | Tommy · Tiger | Ursula · Uakari monkey | Vicky · Vole

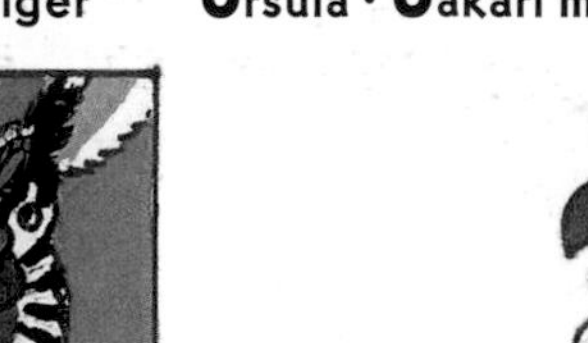

Wanda · Wolf | Xavier · Xenosaurus | Yolanda · Yak | Zach · Zebra | CoCo · Cockatoo

Miss Bindergarten
Border collie

Mrs. Simpson
Suricate

Mr. King
Penguin

Mrs. Leo
Leopard

Nurse Nelson
Nyala

Ms. Chavez
Chimpanzee

Carl Cox
Coyote